TRIG
SEES
RED

TRIG SEES RED

BY
ROBERT NEWTON PECK

c.1

Illustrated by Pamela Johnson

Little, Brown and Company

BOSTON   TORONTO

Second Printing

T 09/78

Library of Congress Cataloging in Publication Data

Peck, Robert Newton.
  Trig sees red.

  SUMMARY: An official Junior G-man takes matters into her own hands when Clodsburg's only uniformed policeman is replaced by a traffic light.
  [1. Humorous stories]   I. Johnson, Pamela.
II. Title.
PZ7.P339Tt   [Fic]   78-18348
ISBN 0-316-69656-0

HOR

Published simultaneously in Canada
by Little, Brown & Company (Canada) Limited

PRINTED IN THE UNITED STATES OF AMERICA

To my children,
Christopher and Anne

1

"COME ON, TRIG."

With a running start I jumped over Jason, who was biting a flea on his tail, so I could catch up to Bud Griffin and head for home. I was a happy girl. School was out for the day, and we always jumped over old Jason whenever we took the shortcut back of Herb Lester's Fix-it Garage.

"Sure is hot for June," I said.

"Yup," Bud agreed, "it certain is."

The two of us stopped to twist the wheel, so we could help ourselves to a drink of water from the Fix-it Garage hose. Herb Lester watched us with well-founded suspicion. It was only last week when we'd aimed the hose at Jason, Mr. Lester's old coonhound, who was asleep at the time and looked hot. Since he was panting, we were only trying to cool him off. But when the water hit him full force, Jason let out a loud howl. Then he jumped up and ran, knocking over a stack of old car tires which rolled off toward all eight points of the compass. But today we just wanted a drink.

"Get away from there!" yelled Mr. Lester.

We ran. Still thirsty, seeing as the hose had been in the sun and the water was hotter than Satan's spit.

Turning the corner behind Jenner's Grocery, all I did was *look* at the oranges in a bin out front. And that's all Bud did was *look*.

"Don't get any notions," warned Mr. Jenner, wiping his hands on a dirty white apron, and placing his gaunt body between us and his fruit.

I heard a car blow its horn.

"Come on," I said to Bud, "let's cross over."

Lots of cars toot at Six Corners, which is smack dab in the middle of the town of Clodsburg. That's because our three main streets all intersect there, like a six-leg spider, and it was usually busy that time of the day. But busier today. Horns were blowing and a few drivers had stuck their heads out of the windows in order to yell to the cars ahead of them to hurry up. But not many cars were moving. Not an inch.

"Hey," said Bud, "where's old Pop?"

Pop Copperskittle was Clodsburg's only uniformed police officer. As he'd been the town cop for over fifty years, everybody knew Pop. He was the kind of gent who'd blow his silver whistle to let a cat cross the street, especially if she held a kitten in her mouth. Some people didn't like Pop the Cop, but I sure did.

Lots of people, mostly grown-ups, said that Pop Copperskittle was blinder than a bat, deaf as a door-nail, and lame as a duck. But I specially liked Pop whenever he'd blow his whistle at some impatient motorist. Six Corners was the busiest crossing in town, and Pop would often yell out: "S'matter? Ya got ants in your pants? Wait yer dang turn!" Maybe some folks

4

claimed that Pop was grumpy, but he always smiled at me.

So when I saw Six Corners, yet didn't see Pop, I sort of got myself mad all over again. To look at the crossing at Six Corners and not see Pop Copperskittle was next to looking at our Town Square and not seeing the red cannon. Clodsburg wouldn't be the same town without our big cannon in the square. Even though the Town Square was really a triangle.

"I reckon you heard the bad news."

"What news?" Bud asked me.

"They fired Pop the Cop."

Bud lifted his eyebrows. "Honest?"

"If I'm lying," I said, "I hope I turn blue and throw up breakfast," which is something I always say. I learned it from my Uncle Fred, who's a real sport when it comes to conversation.

"Pop lost his job?" Bud asked.

"He sure did," I said, kicking an empty tobacco can. It rattled against a downspout and then lay quiet. "And I don't like it. Not one pinch."

"Gee," said Bud, "old Pop's one of the best."

I nodded. "Pop's the kind of guy who'd bend over and lift a bug out a puddle."

As we stood there, along came elderly Miss Beekin who still gave lessons on the pianola, walking hip to hip with a gentleman of like vintage, Reverend Toop of the Baptist Church.

"It's a crime," said Miss Beekin. Her voice crackled sort of like an old chicken.

"You can say *that* again, Miss Beekin."

"A *crime* and downright shameful."

My ears perked up. Crime?

"It's not *human* to let officer Copperskittle go, after all the years he's kept peace in this town."

"You're right, Miss Beekin," said Reverend Toop, "and that's the only word for it. Firing Pop is a crime!"

A *crime*?

I watched the Reverend Toop and Miss Beekin limp slowly down the street. They turned into Conron's Drugs and stopped, as they so often did, to browse at the liniment counter.

Meanwhile, beneath the crossing at Six Corners, horns continued to blast louder and louder. I smiled.

"This'll wake up Clodsburg," I said.

"That racket would fetch back the dead," said Bud.

"No, I meant about Pop."

"Like what, Trig?"

"Well, when Mayor Swagg and the Town Council hear all the clatter and see the ruckus that gets kicked up when there's nobody to direct traffic, they'll change their dumb minds and rehire Pop."

"No," said Bud.

"No?"

"I heard some news, too."

"Such as?"

"I overheard Mayor Swagg's cousin."

"The one he calls Cousin Swade?"

"Yeah," said Bud, "that's the guy."

"He's the County Traffic Commissioner, isn't he?"

"That's the one."

"So what'd he have to say?"

"Swade Swagg said there's to be a hanging."

"To hang what?"

"I don't know. All I heard Swade Swagg say was that they'd hang it tomorrow, on Saturday."

"Yikes," I said, "I never seen a hanging. Have you, Bud?"

"No, but I don't guess they're going to hang a person. Leastwise, it didn't sound that way to *my* ear."

A *hanging,* I was thinking. Try as I might, I couldn't seem to wash the picture or the word out of my mind. Life sure was about to turn exciting here in Clodsburg. There was more in the air than just the smell of the glue factory.

"Nope," said Bud again, "they don't aim to hang a person."

"What are they going to hang?" I asked.

"A *thing.*"

2

"OKAY," I said. "Hands up."

Because I was the leader, Bud Griffin and Skip Warner raised their right hands, and were prepared to be sworn in. I let both boys stand there, underneath the dead hickory tree behind Charlie Dingo's outhouse, while I pinned an official G-man badge on Bud and then on Skip.

"Ow!" Skip jumped. "You stuck me, Trig."

"Sorry," I said. "But to be a Junior G-man, you gotta get used to hardship, just like Mr. Melvin Purvis."

I was already wearing my *own* badge, and had wore

it all spring. And it sure took the three of us long enough to save up twenty-one Soppie box tops to send away and trade for our three "artificial silver badges made from genuine plastite." Soppies tasted a little better than chewing up a milk-soaked mattress, and the badges were smaller than they appeared on the back of a box of Soppie breakfast cereal, but at least they were official.

"Repeat after me," I said. "Upon my honor . . . I hereby promise to uphold the legal statutes of the United States of America . . . and to pursue with dedication . . . all criminals and fugitives . . . from law and order. Don't just stand there, you guys. Put your hands down."

"Trig . . ."

"Yeah?"

"What the deuce is a statute?"

"Well," I scratched the bug bite on my hip, "I reckon it's like a statue, but it's big and made out of granite or marble. And it stands up in a park to honor some famous hero like George Washington. I guess that's a statute."

"How come you have to *uphold* it?"

"Because," I told Skip, "if'n ya don't, the pesky statute's liable to topple over in a sudden breeze and bust itself up into bits."

"Yeah," said Bud, "ya wouldn't want to see George Washington's head all by his lonesome, would ya? Or his sword all busted?"

"I don't guess I would," said Skip.

"That," I told Skip and Bud, "concludes our pledging ceremony. Now comes the good part."

"Like what?"

"The initiation."

"You didn't say there'd be *that*," said Bud.

"No, I don't guess I told you guys about the initiation, but for a very good reason."

"What reason?"

I picked up my official Melvin Purvis Junior G-man machine gun, holding it under one arm, its dangerous barrel pointed downward. "Men, there won't be many secrets between us. Leastwise, not often. However, at times I just can't tell you guys *everything* in advance."

"How come?"

"For reasons of security," I said.

Slowly I pulled back the lever of my machine gun, allowing both Bud and Skip to hear every darn click, until my tommy gun was fully cocked. My finger teased the trigger, while Bud and Skip held their breath, expecting an ear-shattering burst of sound that only a gun of such caliber could make. My weapon may have been less than a real gun, but to me it sure was more than a toy.

"First off," I said, "each new member is required to demonstrate his physical skill."

"And do what?"

"According to my leader's manual," I said . . .

"Funny thing, Trig, but we never get to *see* that manual you claim you got."

"You will," I said, "in due course."

"When?"

"Sometime *after* you guys get initiated."

"What we gotta do?"

"First thing, you have to jump Alf's Crick."

"Jump across it?"

"Yup."

"Where at?" Bud asked me.

"Best place," I said, "to jump Alf's Crick is between the muskrat humps and where Mrs. Rixbee hangs out her wash."

"And that's the widest part," said Skip.

Bud said, "Yeah, and the deepest."

"I didn't write the manual," I said.

"Who did?"

"Mr. Melvin Purvis," I said, giving my gun a gentle but convincing pat, like I was trying to quiet her down before she went off and blasted the head off every buttercup in Vermont.

"Well," said Bud, "*we* can jump across."

Skip, who was about as chubby as Bud was lean, didn't look so sure.

"Come on, men."

Taking the downhill path, we crawled under Pick Wilson's fence and then ran through his garden, not much of which was up yet. Pick chased us away with his hoe. Mrs. Rixbee sort of did likewise with her broom as we ducked between a pair of wet bedsheets. It sure was, I thought as we ran, unpopular to be a kid.

"There she be," sighed Bud.

"Alf's Crick."

I always wondered who Alf was, seeing as the crick was named after him; yet nobody in Clodsburg ever seemed to know. Alf's Crick was hardly a very important waterway. Not like the Panama Canal or anything like that. Yet my mother talked a lot about it: "You stay away from Alf's Crick," was what she often said. Hardly a day went by without her saying it. Bud and Skip and I spent a lot of time hanging around the crick until it dried up every August.

But now it was June. Melted snow and springtime rain had made the crickbed into pools and rapids, filled with foam, frogs, fish and old auto tires. Once I'd found the springs of an old cot, sort of rusty, that made my hands all brown by the time I dragged it home. Mama didn't want it. All it needed was a few slaps of fresh paint. She made me drag it all the way across the back pasture to the dump.

"Men," I said, as my careful eye searched out a pair of banks that were far enough apart that a buck deer couldn't have jumped from one to the other, "that there is the proper spot."

"You *sure*, Trig?"

I nodded. "According to the manual."

"Nobody could jump *that*," said Skip.

"Jumping across is not the most important thing," I said. "Not at all."

"Who says?"

"Mr. Melvin Purvis," I said, "that's who."

"He ain't ever been here to Clodsburg."

"No I don't guess he has. I never seen Egypt but I know the pyramids are there. Miss Millerton said that's where they were, only they call *their* crick the Nile."

"Alf's sounds better," said Bud.

"Yeah," I said, "but I bet the Nile runs a shade wider. So just be glad, you men, that you don't have to be a G-man in Egypt. Like I was saying, the important thing is not to jump across, but to *try*."

"Okay," said Bud and Skip.

Skip jumped first and landed in the middle. Soaking wet, he flopped himself to shore and shivered. Bud almost cleared the crick, as he landed in just an inch of water, beneath which was four feet of mud.

"Close," I said.

3

"BEST WE HURRY," I suggested.

Skip was still wet, and Bud muddy, at the time we cut behind the gristmill and through the lumber yard into town. Saturday morning was usual beehive busy, and this particular day was no exception.

"Gee," said Skip, "seems like everybody in the whole county's come to Clodsburg."

Skip was right.

"Trig . . ."

"Yeah?"

"Let's go to the hanging."

"That," I said, not quite sure of where or what the hanging would be, "is just what we aim to do."

"Honest?"

"Yup," I said, "because it's part of your initiation ceremony."

"It is?"

I nodded, my mouth set grim and firm. "Ya see," I told them, "I sort of figured that a genuine *hang* would be just what the doctor ordered to give you men some experience."

"Huh? What doctor?"

"The doctor that ordered the hanging," I said.

Skip scratched his butt. "I thought a *judge* did that."

I nodded. "Sometimes they do."

"Trig, you sure know a lot about law and cricks and statutes and stuff."

"All in the manual," I said.

Things sure were hopping at Six Corners. Cars were tooting at each other while angry motorists exchanged insults: "Slow poke!" yelled a man to the lady driver in the car in front of his.

Her answer was prompt. "I may be slow, Henry, but I'm ahead of *you*."

I saw Feldon Jessup up on the roof of his Ford, standing in his stocking feet. I reckon he'd pulled off his work boots so's he wouldn't scratch the paint. He stared with his mouth open.

Somebody yelled up to Feldon to ask him what he could see.

"Nothin' yet. Nothin' *to* see."

"Where they aim to hang it?"

"Well," said Feldon, "I reckon right up yonder in the middle and dead center. That's what they usual do."

"How'd *you* know?"

"On account," Feldon Jessup explained, "of me and the Mrs. took the Ford down to Rutland a year ago. Fair time. And we saw one of them fancy electric contraptions. With our own eyes."

"You and Doris *saw* one?"

"Sure did."

Skip and Bud and I edged a bit closer, to share the wisdom that Feldon Jessup seemed ready to impart.

"You mean you saw a real *traffic light?*"

Feldon nodded. "Dangest thing you ever see. Me and the Mrs. must of stood there for near an hour, just watching it blink."

"What color was it?"

Feldon Jessup raised a finger. "That's the whole beauty of the thing. It just hung up there in the air, red . . . yeller . . . green."

"All at the same time?"

"No! I should say *not,*" said Feldon.

"You sure?"

"Course I'm sure. A doohinky like that ain't something a body is fixed to forget right soon. A traffic light is one heck of a sight to see."

"Was it pretty?"

"Well," said Feldon, "it weren't exactly Christmas Eve, or near to, but I tell you that I dang near had to drag Doris back to where we'd hitched the Ford. She'd a stood and stared at that traffic light all day and near to milking. And you know that Doris ain't the type of woman who gets amused that easy."

Mrs. Jessup, I then recalled, was a local lady who'd often stand outside the barbershop and look into the window so she could watch Norm Gibbard cut hair. She was also in the very front row at the hardware store the day that city-fella gave the demonstration to show how a thermos bottle worked: "The coffee goes in hot," the man had said, "and an hour later it's still hot. And when ice tea goes in cold, she *stays* cold until you drink it."

"My stars," Doris had said as she'd pointed at the thermos, "you wouldn't believe a bottle would taste the difference. How's it know?"

We heard a truck beep its horn so it wouldn't run over a scatter of chickens that were pecking away at the dust in the road. So we all turned to watch the arrival of the truck. As it passed by me and sort of squeaked to a stop, I recognized the driver, who was the mayor's cousin, Swade Swagg.

"Here it comes," said Feldon.

In the back of the truck was a large box, which was

soon opened up with wire snippers and a crowbar. Carefully, cautiously, the many gifted fingers of Clodsburg lifted the contraption up from the box. Whatever it was, it sure was yellow as corn.

Doris Jessup poked her nose too close, and so Swade Swagg asked her to back off an inch or two, and give the contraption "room to breathe." As he mentioned breathing, I notice that Doris seemed not to be doing any of her own.

Out it came.

"Stand back, folks," said Mayor Swagg. "These here do-dads are electric cables, and even though they ain't hooked up, there just might be a lick or two of juice left inside. Enough to fry a body like an egg."

The crowd dispersed faster than feathers in a wind.

No octopus ever had as many arms and legs as Clodsburg's new traffic light. It took a full day to untangle all the twists and turns. We got tired just standing there hour after hour. I thought my arches would ache off. In fact, it took so long to get the darn thing hung that even Doris Jessup had to go sit herself down on a park bench. We never went home to supper. Bud and Skip and I just sort of stood there and watched Swade Swagg argue with his nephew, Honus. The sun went down and lights went on all over Clodsburg, except for the traffic light, which stayed darker than nobody home.

"Okay," a man yelled, "she's connected."

My neck hurt from looking up into the air as the new traffic light swayed to and fro above Six Corners.

"Stand back, folks."

We stood back, not daring to speak or breathe, as Mayor Swagg stepped forward to "throw the switch" as somebody said.

"Where's he aim to throw it?" I asked, but no one volunteered to answer. We all leaned forward, mouths open, silent as sheep watching a dog . . . as the official thumb of Mayor Swagg rested on the switch.

"Ready?" asked the mayor. He looked more nervous than a fly in a bass drum.

Doris Jessup said "ready."

"Not you, Doris. I was talking to Cousin Swade."

"We been *ready* all day," she snorted.

"Here goes!" yelled Mayor Swagg.

He "threw" the switch. Sparks popped from the traffic light. But it lit up! We all cheered. And I had to admit that Feldon Jessup had been right. Our new traffic light did change color . . . about three times every second . . . green red green red green.

"Hmm," muttered the mayor, "she seems to be on the fritz. Hey, I wonder what this other little switch is for."

Before anyone could stop him, Mayor Swagg "threw" that one, too. The traffic light sort of coughed, turned purple, and then exploded in a great puff of orange smoke. It also blew out every light in Clodsburg.

"Well," said Mayor Swagg in the dark, "so that's what the other switch does."

4

"GOT A MATCH?" somebody asked.

"Yeah, I got a perfect match. Your brains and my jackass."

"Someone go get Herb Lester."

"Where is he?"

"Move off my foot, ya big horse, and maybe I can show ya."

We were all sort of milling around in the dark, as several of the men in charge took turns shouting at each other. Mayor Swagg pointed at Cousin Swade who pointed at his nephew, Honus, who pointed at Doris Jessup. That was when a careless boot stepped on Jason's tail and he leaped up and bit Mayor Swagg on the rump.

"Dang that dumb dog!" he said. "Whose is it?"

"Mine," said Herb Lester, "and you can fix your own dumb stoplight."

"Now just keep your shirt on, Herb," said Mayor Swagg. "I didn't mean that Jason was dumb. You know my reputation for being kind to dumb animals."

"There! You called him *dumb* again."

"Well, you called my traffic light dumb, didn't you?"

"Looks pretty dumb to me," said Herb, "and what's more, Pop Copperskittle is related to my wife's first cousin."

"I didn't know that."

"Huh," snorted Herb as he looked up at the traffic light. "Seems there's plenty you boys don't know."

"Can you fix it?"

"Sure can. I can fix a traffic light faster than you can fix a traffic ticket."

"Best you show some respect," said Mayor Swagg, keeping his backside to the wall as old Jason growled.

As it was Saturday night, people kept arriving in town, more folks than Clodsburg could possibly hold. Six Corners was a tangle of irate motorists and honking horns.

"What do you think, Trig?" asked Bud.

"Serves 'em right," I said. "Now maybe they'll see how important Pop is. Poor old Pop the Cop. I don't guess the three of us ought to sit back and not get even."

"How?" asked Skip.

"Yeah," said Bud. "What'll we do, Trig?"

"Well," I said, "I got an idea."

"Spill it."

"Okay, maybe we write a letter to Mr. Melvin Purvis." As I said it, I puffed a breath of air on my Junior G-man badge and shined it with the hem of my dress.

"But," said Bud, "by the time he gets our letter and writes back some orders, it'll be too late."

"And," said Skip, "next Tuesday is the big day, the eleventh of June."

Swagg Day, and not a kid in Clodsburg didn't know about it. We never had school on that day, on account of what happened in Clodsburg back on 11 June 1777, when Iscariot Swagg fired off the cannon to warn the settlement that the British were coming.

"I reckon," said Bud, "they'll shoot off the cannon again this year."

"Sure," I said, "come Tuesday."

We heard Herb Lester say that he was going to fetch his long ladder. Mr. Jessup offered to help. The three of us kids decided to take ourselves a seat. Like three on a horse, we straddled the big cool barrel of the red cannon in the Town Square, and waited.

"Make way," yelled Herb Lester, who, along with Feldon Jessup at the other end, toted a long ladder to a spot in the exact center of town, directly beneath Clodsburg's newest electronic marvel.

"Somebody unplug it," ordered Herb.

"It is," said Mayor Swagg. "I think."

Up the ladder Herb climbed, higher and higher, causing the necks of all citizens to stretch and all mouths to open. Perched as we were on the red cannon, the three of us could see right well. With a flashlight in his left hand and a screwdriver in his right, Mr. Lester began to tinker with the blinker, with the skilled hands and mechanical training that only Clodsburg could produce.

Sparks popped! And real colorful.

Yet no more colorful than the purple words and phrases that popped from the lips of a shocked Herb Lester. He dropped the flashlight. Like a comet, down it fell in a tailspin. Mr. Jessup was below, holding the ladder, and the flashlight landed on his nose, which prompted cuss words from both ends of the ladder. Picking up the flashlight, Mr. Jessup threw it back up to Mr. Lester, as hard as he could. And then Herb hollered; which caused his coondog, Jason, to again bite Mayor Swagg on the rump. The mayor kicked at the dog, and missed, but his foot met Doris Jessup's shin. That was when she swung her umbrella like a baseball bat. But the mayor ducked. The umbrella whacked the ear of the Reverend Toop, who mentioned God.

Leaving the ladder to hold itself as well as Herb Lester up on top, Feldon Jessup ran over to quiet his wife, with little success. Everyone was yelling.

"Boy," said Bud, "this sure is fun."

"Better than a movie," I said.

"Sure is," said Skip.

Jason seemed to be having the most fun, as he ran from person to person, trying to bite every backside in Clodsburg. Doris Jessup was the only one who had the gumption to try and bite him back. Lots of horns honked but not even one car budged an inch, except for Orrin Dillard's pickup truck. It appeared Orrin sort of got a mite mixed up with his gear shifting and threw her into reverse, because he backed into one leg of the ladder.

"Look out!" somebody yelled out.

The ladder was launched straight up with Herb Lester clinging to the very top rung; then it started a backward arch and tossed poor Herb through the upstairs window of Ransom's Boarding House. Miss Ivy Ransom, its proprietor, took in only female boarders of spinster status. That was why, as I heard and saw Herb Lester shatter the glass, I sort of got to wondering whose bedroom he'd just entered.

Then we heard a scream.

A moment later I saw Herb trying to climb *out* the broken window. Behind him, I recognized Miss Beekin, the elderly pianola teacher, hitting Herb with a red rubber toilet plunger. Her face was even redder than her weapon. Folks around town always said that she had the temper of a wet cat. Herb started down the top of the ladder; not too simple a feat in the dark when you're being screamed at plus bopped with a toilet plunger.

"Peeping Tom!" yelled Miss Beekin.

"This," I said to Skip and Bud, "has got to be about the best old Saturday night I ever spent."

"Yeah," said Skip, "I wouldn't trade this for a whole week of Sundays."

"All part of the initiation," I said.

Skip's fat face looked real serious. "You mean you *planned* all this, Trig?"

"All in the manual," I said. "And the best part is . . . as long as we live, we'll never have to eat even one more Soppie."

Bud and Skip and I laughed so hard we fell off the barrel of the red cannon.

5

OUR FUN stopped soon after.

Mama and Aunt Helena appeared on the scene and snaked me home. I had to take a bath and was marched straight off for bed.

But then on Sunday afternoon, I met Bud and Skip down in our pasture and we legged it into town to take a close look-see at what was left of the mess. Herb Lester's ladder was leaning against Ransom's Boarding House like it was still too tuckered out from Saturday night to do much else. And mean old Jason was there, too, looking for one more bottom to bite. He curled his lip at us.

The new traffic light was working. Red, then green, with a flash of yellow in between. But the only soul we saw looking up at it was old Pop Copperskittle. He just sort of stood there, without his uniform, staring up at the new contraption and scratching his white hair.

"Hi Pop," we all chirped.

"Hey there, kids. How's tricks?"

"It's a *crime*," I said to Pop.

"What is?"

"Your getting fired. I hate that old traffic light. And I sure hope it goes on the fritz every Saturday night."

Pop said, "Well, I don't."

"You *don't*?"

"Nope. Let 'em have it. Maybe it's high time Clodsburg went modern like the rest of the world."

"Honest?"

"Yup," said Pop. "I'm about as up-to-date and new-fangled as a buggy whip." He shook his head. "Guess it's about time I took off my badge and put on slippers."

Grunting as though his backbone was stiff, Pop sat himself down on a bench in the park, right near the big red cannon, while the three of us sprawled on the grass at his feet. His shoes were old and worn out. It had been a long time since those shoes had either danced up a jig or even sported a two-bit shine. One of his laces had busted and had been knotted up short. The other lace looked near as ragged.

"I'm used up," sighed Pop.

As I looked at him, forcing my face to grin, Pop reached down and touched my cheek with the back of his knuckles. And then it was his turn to smile.

"Elizabeth Trigman, I recall the day you got yourself born," he said to me.

"You do?"

Pop nodded. "Bet yer boots I do. Right there I was, directing traffic, when Grace Fullerman give a whoa to her horse in order to tell me the news."

"What'd she say?"

"As I recollect, she said . . . 'Charlie Trigman's got himself a daughter.'"

"You really remember?"

"Hope to jump a stump. Seems like it was only yesterday. And what's more, I even recall when these two cussed cohorts of yours got born." Pop nodded at Skip and Bud. Then he looked back at me. "Trig, you was the handsomest babe I ever laid eyes on. Pretty as Christmas."

"Hard to believe," said Bud, who put a hand over his mouth like he had to throw up.

"I even recollect the day yer *ma* was born. She was a MacDonald and they all lived out on the old Gilbert Hill road. That right?"

"Right as rain," I said. "My ma was a MacDonald before she was a Trigman."

"Pop," asked Skip, "did you ever get married?"

"Me? Nope, that's about the one and only mistake I ever made. Wish I had of."

Picking up a fallen twig, Pop cracked open his jackknife and then squinted along the wood, measuring it with his good eye. Drawing the blade into his thumb, he started to undress the bark. It fell in little gray and orange curls between his old shoes.

"Whatcha makin, Pop?" asked Bud.

"Nothing. I'm just shaving away the time."

Across the green a truck halted. I recognized it as Orrin Dillard's blue pickup. Then another car stopped. Some men got out. Mayor Swagg was among them. They had several balls of what looked to me like heavy white twine, the kind that's too worthless lean for a clothesline and too thick for a kite. From the bin of the pickup, I saw Orrin lift up a burlap bag and then empty out a whole mess of stakes. Mayor Swagg squatted and pointed and told everybody, like always, just what he wanted 'em to do.

"I wonder what's up," I said.

Pop just snorted. If he knew what the men were doing

with twine and stakes, he sure was keeping it a real secret.

"Do you know what they're doing?" I asked Pop.

The old man just snorted. "Course I do."

"Tell us."

"Go ask, if yer so all-fussed curious. Waste of time is what it is. Dumbest tomfool game ever invented by man or demon."

"A *game*?"

"Some call it that. As for me, I'd a whole lot druther pitch horseshoes against a three-legged hinny than play *that* game."

"Which game?"

Pop snorted. "You'll soon see."

"Baseball?" asked Bud.

"Nope," said Pop.

"Football?"

"Neither one. And I can't say I cotton to either one of *them,* neither. But I know what they're setting up, and in my opinion it be a sorry way to fill up leisure. That there *game,* if you can call it that, is not even a pure and simple waste of good grass."

"Grass?"

"Yup. They'd all be further ahead if'n they took that same grass and spoon-fed a heifer."

Pop gave his nose a healthy snuff, looking first at the new red light and then across the park to where Mayor Swagg was doing his best to untangle a mess of string. The twine was so snarled up that it looked more like an ostrich nest. I sort of expected to see an egg the size of a football fall out.

"Pull," said Orrin Dillard. As he spoke he gave his end of the string a yank.

"Confound it," said Mayor Swagg, "we won't ever untangle it, Orrin, unless you quit your tugging the thing."

"I say we cut it."

"No!"

"Well, why not?"

"Because we need all that's here to lay out the lanes, that's why. Boy," said Mayor Swagg, "I sure would give

anything to know the dumb gink who rolled this string back up last year."

"I *know* who did it."

"Who?" asked Mayor Swagg.

"You did."

Mayor Swagg threw the tangle of string down on the grass and stomped on it. About nine times. Mopping his brow with a rag, he then picked up the string. By accident, Orrin yanked it out of his hands.

"Darn you, Orrin."

"I didn't do nothing."

"No," said Mayor Swagg, "and you never will."

"Untangle it your own self if'n you're so blessed smart."

"I intend to. And you don't have a call to get so fired up. To untangle any mess you first have to keep a cool head."

"And stomp it?"

"Dang it, Orrin . . . you mind your end of the string and I'll tend to mine."

"Suits me."

"And don't yank *my* part."

"I'll yank if I darn please."

Orrin Dillard yanked harder than ever, which prompted Mayor Swagg to respond, yanking with both his chubby hands clenching what looked near to a mile of string.

The knots tightened. So did nerves.

"Bowling," said Pop.

6

Dear Mrs. Purvis;

My name is Elizabeth Taigman but my pals call me Trig for short and we sort of got to wondering if you could help us solve a crime here in Clodsburg that got started because Pop got fired and the new light didn't work and blew out all the fuzes so bad that some folks said the town won't ever be the same but if you think the string is all tangled up you should see our electrick wires which now sort of drooop across the street at Six Corners and up fixed to the roof ~~of~~ of Miss Ivy Ransom's Boarding House where Miss Beekin resides with her toilet plunger and won't let Herb Lester into her room which is OK by me because his dog bit our mayor on the rump and he never did let us get a drink of water very much. Your freind, Trig

"That oughta do it," I said, licking the envelope, which was addressed to Mr. Melvin Purvis in care of Soppies at Battle Creek, Michigan.

"It sure should," said Bud.

"Come on," I said to Bud and Skip, "and we'll mail it."

School had just let out (Miss Millerton had taken her usual two tablets of Anacin) and the three of us were sort of strolling down Main Street. As I slipped my letter into a mailbox, which was painted the color of an olive with no red bellybutton, I looked across the street. Mayor Swagg was emerging from the Clodsburg Post Office, holding a package. The box was a cubic foot, adorned with brown wrapping paper, and tied up with sturdy string.

"It's here," hollered Mayor Swagg.

As he smiled down at the box he was toting, he near to run smack into Feldon Jessup. Feldon, who was tall and hungry, looked sort of silly beside Mayor Swagg, who was short and well-fed.

"Here it is," said the mayor again.

"What's it be?"

"Oh," said Mayor Swagg, "I can't wait to open her up. Cuss this string. I can't break it."

"Here's a knife."

Feldon held the box while Mayor Swagg quickly cut the string; and then, with anxious fingers, tore open the many layers and leaves of brown paper. Out came the prize.

"It's a ball," said Feldon.

Bud and Skip and I walked over to get ourselves more of a closer look-see.

"Oh, oh, oh," said the mayor, "I'm just too excited to breathe. Finally it came. My shiny new red bowling ball. I can't wait for the new bowling alley to come to town, now that I got my ball."

"Too bad," said Mr. Jessup.

"Too bad about what?"

"Well, near as I can see, that ball of yours would be okay, but it's got two holes in it. Maybe it's one of them *factory rejects* that you can get for half price."

"Holes! That's a hot one, Feldon. Don't you know *anything* about bowling? These holes are where I stick my . . ."

"Maybe you could plug 'em with putty."

"How else would I roll the ball? The holes are *supposed* to be exactly where they be. One for my middle finger and one for my thumb. They're part of the ball."

"Huh? I never figured a *hole* was part of anything."

"Well, it is," said Mayor Swagg. "See?"

"Them holes look a bit *small* to me," said Feldon. "You sure it'll be a proper fit?"

"Of course I'm sure. I had this here red ball special made. Sent 'em the measurements and all. I even specified the weight and color. Marble red."

"If you ask me, Mayor, you'll never squeeze *your* chubby fingers into holes as tiny as the ones I'm looking at."

"Poppycock! Here, I'll show ya the proper grip, Feldon, so the next time folks talk bowling, you'll know a thing or two. I'll stick my fingers in the holes. You hold the ball."

"Okay."

"See! A real snug fit."

"Got it?" Without waiting for an answer, Feldon Jessup let loose and the ball fell, landing on his toe. Mayor Swagg was suddenly bent over, as if trying to pick up the ball by its holes. Mr. Jessup danced around, shaking his foot, and using some colorful terms that might have something to do with bowling.

"Oh, my *toe!*"

What happened next sure was a surprising sight. Before the mayor could recover and straighten up, or yank his fingers out of the ball, Mr. Jessup sort of lost his temper. Drawing back his good foot, he kicked the mayor's red bowling ball with his work boot. Real hard. The kick spun Mayor Swagg around about three full turns while the ball swung away outside him in three wide circles.

"Ahhhh!" screamed the mayor.

"You broke my *toe!*" yelled Feldon.

"My *thumb,*" cried the mayor. "I think I heard it crack! Darn you, Jessup. Don't you know enough not to never *kick* a bowling ball?"

"And don't you know enough not to *drop* one on somebody's toe?"

"Don't just stand there. Lend me a hand and we'll stuff my ball back into its box before it gets scratched."

Slowly, the two men reboxed the red bowling ball. But even then, for some strange reason, Mayor Swagg didn't seem to release his hold on his newest possession.

"S'matter?"

"It's my thumb."

"What about it?"

"My doggone thumb is swelling. I don't seem to be able to pull it out. Dang it! Ouch! Holy Hannah, it hurts like all festering fury."

"Just give her a good yank."

"Be quiet, Jessup. I certainly know enough to put my thumb in my own bowling ball."

"Yup," agree Mr. Jessup, "you know enough for that."

7

"HIGHER," I whispered.

Bud and Skip were bending over, hip to hip, while I stood on their backs, trying to sneak a peek into Doc Ellerby's rear window. There was grit on the sill which didn't bother me a whole lot, seeing as my hands were even blacker.

"What's he doing?" Bud whispered.

"I can't make it out."

"How come?"

"Because the window's dirty. Or my glasses."

"Our backs are going to be dirtier after you get through scuffing your muddy sneakers all over us."

"A good G-man never complains," I said, breathing on the window pane and then wiping it into sort of a gray smudge.

"Who says?"

"I read it in the manual."

"Hurry up, Trig," said Skip, "and tell us what's going on inside."

"Well," I said, "Doc is sitting on his side of the desk with Mayor Swagg on the other. And now Doc just hooked up his stethoscope into his ears and he's putting the funnel end on the bowling ball."

"Why in tarnation," said our impatient mayor, "are you listening to my bowling ball?"

"You said you heard a crack," said Doc.

"Yeah, but it weren't the ball. It was my doggone blessed busted thumb. It hurts like all Hades."

"Well, you probably sprained it. Let me get my head mirror adjusted so's I can examine it real thorough."

"How are you fixing to examine my thumb when you can't even see it?"

"Don't tell *me* how to practice medicine. Try to unplug your thumb and let me have a close look at it."

"Doggone you, Doc. I just got through explaining about the Post Office and how Feldon Jessup kicked my ball. I *can't* get my thumb out. It's stuck fast."

"My opinion is . . . your thumb's swelling up."

"What'll I do?"

I saw Doc slowly reach out and grab the bowling ball. "Sometimes, in cases such as this, the practical thing to do is either leave it alone. Or, give it a good YANK!"

"Yyyaaaahhhhh!" screamed the mayor.

"Is it loose?"

"No, you old jackass. It ain't loose at all. The only thing *loose* around here is one of the screws in your brain. Why'd you have to yank it?"

"Now keep calm," Doc advised.

"Keep *calm?*"

"Best you do. These things can turn serious."

"My thumb's sprained. Now it's probable busted. And it's all *your* fault."

"*My* fault? I didn't stick your stupid thumb in a bowling ball. Only a dang fool would do that."

"Well, then it's Feldon's fault."

"If you want my medical opinion . . ."

"That's why I'm here."

"Your thumbs are too fat."

"Some doctor *you* are. There you sit, behind your high and mighty desk, calling people fools and telling a patient that he's got a fat thumb."

"Well, you do."

"What *you* ought to have is a fat lip."

"Cool down, Mayor."

"How in the name of holy can I cool down with this pesky *thing* stuck on my thumb?"

"I think we best x-ray it."

"To look for a fracture?"

38

"That's possible."

Mayor Swagg raised up his free hand to level a finger at Doc Ellerby. "Doc, you wouldn't know a fracture from a hangnail."

"Oh, I wouldn't, eh?"

Doc made a quick grab for the ball just before the mayor jerked it back. And when the ball fell off the desk it cracked Mayor Swagg on the knee. He let out a whoop. "*Yikes!*"

"Quiet," ordered Doc, "or else every person in Clodsburg will think I torture my patients."

"What's happening, Trig?" asked Bud.

"Yeah," chimed in Skip. "How come you don't give *us* two a look?"

With my hand over my mouth, I was trying not to laugh. Even as I peeked through the window pane, I could see that Doc's face and Mayor Swagg's face were both coloring up to be near as red as the mayor's new bowling ball.

"Well," said Doc as he pulled his eyeglasses down to the end of his pointed nose, "you don't have to be a genius to see what *your* trouble is."

"Like what?"

"Plain as day. You see this here *other* hole? The *empty* one?"

"Of course I see it," said the mayor.

Using a ruler on his desk, Doc measured first the empty hole and then the full one. "Ah, just as I thought. Mayor, it appears to me that all you did was stick your thumb in the wrong hole."

"Horse feathers!"

"See for yourself. Trouble with you, Mayor, is that you can't tell a thumb hole from . . . a hole in the ground. Ha!"

"Is that so? Well, let me tell *you* a thing or two, Ellerby. I happen to know a darn sight more about bowling than *you* do about . . ."

"Surgery?"

Mayor Swagg's face turned color faster than Clodsburg's new traffic light, like he'd suddenly threw a switch to change his face from red to yellow. Lips trembling, he whispered his next word: "Surgery?"

Doc's wife entered her husband's office, took herself one look at Mayor Swagg's thumb in the bowling ball, and busted out laughing. "Ha! Ho! Ha-dee-ha! If that ain't the silliest sight, since the parade got rained on, then I'm a monkey's uncle."

"Leave your family out of this," whimpered the mayor.

After she finished laughing, I saw her leave the office and then return, holding a knife. At the tip of its blade rested a yellow gob of something or other, a secret substance that I couldn't quite identify. But when Mayor Swagg saw the knife, up he jumped on Doc's desk, lifting his bowling ball so high that he whacked it against the ceiling.

"No," he hollered. "No surgery."

"Land sakes, all I got is butter."

"Butter?" asked Doc. "Is it suppertime?"

"Hold him," Doc's wife ordered.

"Don't touch me!" yelped Mayor Swagg, jumping off the desk and running for the exit. The mayor got out of the office but the ball didn't. Doc spryly closed the

door on the mayor's wrist. Mayor Swagg was screaming bloody murder; while Doc's wife, Edna, buttered as much of the swollen thumb as the ball would allow. Doc leaned his shoulder against the door and while we all sort of watched and waited, Mayor Swagg's entire hand turned red.

And then purple.

8

"Some gun," said Miss Millerton.

"Thanks," I told our teacher.

"You know, Elizabeth, we could almost shoot off *your* gun today instead of our big red cannon in the Town Square."

"Honest?"

"Sure enough. I've heard you and Skip and Bud talk about this gun so often that I'd certainly feel honored to shoot it myself."

The two of us were standing on the sidewalk just outside Conron's Drugs, as I watched Miss Millerton raise the gun to her shoulder and sight along the barrel. "So this," she finally said, "is an official Melvin Purvis genuine Junior G-man machine gun."

"Certain is," I told her.

"I bet it makes a *real* loud noise."

"So loud," I told Miss Millerton, "that folks would darn near be fixing to muffle their ears if they ever saw my finger anywhere near the trigger."

"Here comes our band," she said.

I looked where she was pointing, and sure enough,

there was the Clodsburg Trombone Assembly strolling toward the grassy triangle in the center of town. About two dozen of our most gifted citizens in the field of martial music. Their pink and silver uniforms sparkled like spit and polish.

"My," said Miss Millerton, "don't they all look splendid. I don't know what this town would do if we didn't have the eleventh day of June to celebrate."

"Yes'm."

Miss Millerton was nuts about history, a subject which I could take not quite as often as mineral oil. She'd told us time and again about what happened on 11 June 1777, the day of Swagg's Rout. A solitary British soldier (ill with pox) had been too ripe to march and was left behind. Quite by chance, he surrounded twenty-seven marksmen of the Clodsburg militia. Yet one escaped to flee in panic: Colonel Iscariot Swagg, who by accident fired off a large cannon. He later explained that he did so to warn Clodsburg that the British were coming.

The British were not coming. They were gone.

But history, according to Miss Millerton, had treated Iscariot Swagg with good fortune; especially the history of Clodsburg written in 1804 by Squire Obediah Swagg and updated in 1913 by Miss Esme Swagg, a local schoolmarm. And, as the English "clerke" tended to add an *e* to every word, Swagg's Rout somehow became Swagg's Route and Colonel Iscariot Swagg — despite the fact that he was flogged for cowardice — became a hero, even if not in his own time.

To the grateful ears of Clodsburg on this day of celebration, the whanging strains of the Clodsburg Trombone Assembly allowed our ears to painfully swell with pride. Our trombonists assembled once a year which, they insisted, rendered rehearsals quite unnecessary. Their best march was *Under the Double Eagle* which they played at least a dozen times, to delight the crowd, adding an audible confetti to this day of days.

"Come on," said Miss Millerton. "I'll treat you to some strawberry ice cream."

As we licked our cones, with small pink streams running down on our knuckles, we watched the bowling on the green. During April and May, the moles of Clodsburg had, as always, turned our bowling green into an obstacle course of humps and bumps. For any ball to reach the pins was a feat in itself, yet no bowler seemed to mind.

"There's the mayor," I said.

"What's that on his thumb? It's white."

"A bandage," I said. "I guess that's the reason he's not bowling this year." I thought I best keep silent on how it happened.

Everyone, like always, had come to town. Colorful balloons were tied to every lamppost and several citizens sold peanuts, popcorn, lemonade, and red candy apples on a stick. Hot dogs abounded. There was hardly a shirt in all of Clodsburg without red, yellow or green . . . from ketchup, mustard or relish. Several kids, overstuffed with goodies, were already throwing up . . . in technicolor.

Swagg Day was in full bloom.

"Well," said Miss Millerton, "I reckon you'll want to

poke around and find your pals, so I'll just go say how-do to your mother and father, and tell them how much better you're doing in geography."

"Yes'm, and thanks for the ice cream."

I watched her go. Miss Millerton looked right pretty in her yellow dress. She sure was the best doggone teacher a kid could have. Miss Millerton was worth looking up to. Sort of like the flag.

Turning about, I spotted Skip and Bud dodging through the crowd on a dead run. Seeing as they were both smiling, I figured some poor devil was in for it. Like they both had "prank" printed on their faces.

"What say, men?"

"We *found* it," said Bud.

"Honest," said Skip. "We just sort of stumbled across it and *there* she was."

"Wow!" I said. "Where *is* it?"

Bud raised an arm and started to point, which made me pull his arm down real sudden, so's we wouldn't telegraph our intentions all over the doggone county for everybody to see. A plan was taking shape in my brain. But I sure didn't want all of Clodsburg to know just what we'd be up to.

"Don't point," I told him.

"No," agreed Skip. "We gotta be real sly."

As we wormed our way through the crowd, I let Bud carry my Junior G-man machine gun, a job he and Skip often fought over. Well, it was okay with me. My gun was darn near as big as I was and it got to feel close as heavy.

"This way," whispered Skip.

We cut behind the feed store, over a fence, and along the roof of the lumber shed . . . until Jake Seaborn yelled to us to fetch ourselves down before we tumbled off and got busted. Our trail came to a halt at the back porch of Mayor Swagg's office. Parked nearby was the mayor's new Model A Ford.

"Where's it hid?" I asked.

"In the rumble seat," Bud answered.

"Yup," said Skip.

I helped myself to a deep breath. "Best we move right easy from here on in," I said.

Climbing up on the rear end of the bright green Ford, I reached for the silver handle, so we could open up the rumble seat. The metal felt hot with June sunshine. The hinges squeaked. But we opened her up and there it was, staring up at us with its two black eyes:

Mayor Swagg's red bowling ball!

"Just like we told ya," said Skip.

"Yeah," said Bud, "we saw the mayor squirrel it away in his rumble seat, like it was some sort of a secret treasure."

"What'll we do with it?" asked Skip.

"On this particular Swagg Day," I said, "Clodsburg is in for one heck of a big shock."

As we lifted the red bowling ball up and out of the mayor's Ford, I let Skip and Bud in on my plan. With mouths open and eyes wide, they listened as I unfolded the details, one by one.

"We'll never get away with it," said Bud.

"But remember, men . . . we're doing this for old Pop, so he can get back his job."

46

"Let's get going," said Skip.

Bud lugged the bowling ball, while Skip packed along my Melvin Purvis machine gun. The timing had to be precise, exactly right.

"Best we be real sneaky," I said, looking at the bowling ball, "or the three of us will get caught. Red handed."

9

"YOU LOOK GREAT," somebody said.

"Thanks," said Marvin Fillput.

Marvin was all decked out in his World War uniform and he looked like a regular soldier. Orange boots, wraparound leggings from his ankles up to his knees, winged britches, topped off by a tin helmet. He was busy saluting near to everyone in town; even the cats and dogs, when nobody was looking.

"Are ya sure you know what you're doing, Marvin?" asked Mayor Swagg.

Marvin rolled the keg marked GUNPOWDER over to a place just in front of the big red cannon.

"Of course I know," Marvin said. "Wasn't I in the Field Artillery?" He started to fill the mouth of the cannon with gunpowder.

"Well," said the mayor, "I s'pose you were if you say so. But all that gunpowder makes me skittery." He started to bite the nail on his thumb even though there was a bandage on it.

"Don't you fret," said Marvin. "When you're a war veteran like I am, you can hold gunpowder like it was no more than a keg of cider."

"Yeah?" said Mayor Swagg. "Well I saw you last Saturday night at the barn dance, and you weren't holding *your* cider so darn steady."

"I was so," said Marvin. He poured more gunpowder into the muzzle of the cannon.

"Was not. I saw you dancing with Mabel Kimmer, kicking up your heels, and stomping all over her feet."

"That's a lie."

"And when Mabel got riled up, you stumbled into the refreshment table, and knocked over the punch bowl. That was when you fell down on top of Huber Gisselgot's fiddle."

"It's not my fault that Mabel Kimmer is such a clumsy

dancer. Besides, if you ask my opinion, the orchestra sounded a whole lot sweeter without Huber's squawky violin."

"Now look, Marvin, I'll have you to know that Huber Gisselgot just happens to be a third cousin of mine."

Marvin said, "Huh! Near everybody in town is a cousin of yours. That's why you're the mayor."

More gunpowder disappeared into the red cannon's mouth. The gun was tipped up and pointing at Six Corners.

"Don't you think," said Mayor Swagg, "that you've put enough powder in for one charge?"

"Nope," said Marvin. He dumped in more.

"We best be cautious or we could blow up the whole town. Are you *sure* you know what you're about? You surely didn't know last Saturday night."

"I did so."

"Herb Lester said that you proposed marriage three times to old Miss Beekin, and once even to him."

"If'n I did I don't remember," said Marvin.

Right then, as Mayor Swagg and Marvin Fillput were continuing to spat, I saw Doris Jessup stroll over to the front end of the big cannon. Up on her tiptoes, she looked into the big black hole.

"What's in there?" she asked.

"Gunpowder," said Marvin.

"To make the cannon shoot?"

"That's right, Doris," said Mayor Swagg.

"Looks pretty full to me," said Doris, "and maybe Marvin put in a pinch too generous."

Marvin turned to Mrs. Jessup and said, "Doris, was you ever in your life a member of the Field Artillery of the United States Army?"

"Nope," said Doris, "but I'm in the Eastern Star."

"Hardly the same," snorted Marvin.

"And," said Doris, "my sister Eunice is a member of the DAR."

"What's that?"

"Daughters of the American Revolution. I don't know too much about it," said Doris, her voice echoing into the mouth of the cannon, "because she's down in Bellows Falls. But I hear they're experts on firearms and like that."

"That don't make *you* an expert."

That was when little old Miss Beekin walked up and poked her umbrella into the cannon's muzzle.

"Careful," said Marvin, "that thing's loaded."

"So, most likely, are you," snarled Miss Beekin. "And I won't marry anyone who can't dance."

Mayor Swagg laughed. "You tell him, Miss Beekin."

"Blame it," said Marvin Fillput, "the trouble with this town is that none of you folks know how to respect a veteran."

Herb Lester joined the group. "Veteran? Marvin, I overheard you did all your soldiering in some army camp out in Oregon."

"I got a nephew in Oregon," said Miss Beekin.

"Doggone it," said Mayor Swagg, "nobody gives a hoot about where you got a nephew or where you don't."

"Golly, I was wrong," said Doris Jessup.

"Huh?"

"Eunice doesn't live in Bellows Falls no more."

"Where does she live?" asked Herb Lester.

"Don't tell!" screeched Miss Beekin. "Don't you tell this Peeping Tom where she lives. Because if he finds out, he'll go sneaking into her window, just like he did mine."

The argument got a bit hotter, and several other people walked over, just to put in their two cents. One of them was Mabel Kimmer.

"Still limping?" asked Marvin Fillput.

Turning around quickly, Mabel glowered at her clumsy dancing partner, and I could see from where we were hiding in the bushes that Mabel wasn't exactly glad to see him.

"If there's anything I can't stand," said Mabel, tossing her head in the air, "it's a man who *sweats* when he dances."

"I don't sweat," said Marvin.

"Huh. Your shirt was soaking wet."

"Well, it wasn't sweat."

"What was it?"

"Cider," said Marvin.

"I recall," said Doris Jessup. "I think Eunice left Bellows Falls and moved out West."

"To where?"

"Down to Oregon. But she didn't mention anything in her letter about the Field Artillery."

"Out there," said Mayor Swagg, "it might be what they call the Coast Artillery."

"How would *you* know?" said Marvin to the mayor.

Herb Lester slapped his thigh. "Ha!"

"I probable know," said Mayor Swagg, "a darn sight more about artillery than *you* do about electric fixing." He pointed his bandaged thumb at Herb.

"Don't stick you thumb in *my* face."

"I'll stick my thumb anywhere I please."

"Yeah," said Doc Ellerby, "and if you want my medical opinion . . ."

"But I'm pretty sure that Eunice *used* to live in Bellows Falls. Now wait. It wasn't Eunice at all. 'Twas my other sister, Sidney, the one that always bumped into things."

Jason came bounding over, wagging his tail, and

jumping up on everybody with his muddy paws until he finally knocked over what was left of the keg of gunpowder.

"There's that awful dog that always looks into my bedroom window," said Miss Beekin.

"That's just old Jason. Belongs to Herb Lester."

"Hmpf," said Miss Beekin. "No wonder."

10

MAYOR SWAGG cleared his throat.

"Folks," he said, "doggone if I can find my new bowling ball. I could swear that I put it in the rumble seat of my car. Did anybody find it? You know me. Always misplacing things. However, it gives me great pleasure, even though I didn't bowl in the contest, to announce this year's winner."

The crowd held its breath.

"Not that it wasn't close," said the mayor, "and it wasn't easy, judging whether or not one of the pins would have turned over even if a certain dumb dog hadn't chased after the ball." Mayor Swagg glowered at Jason who glowered back.

"Who won?" yelled Doris Jessup.

Without answering, the mayor started to unveil the big bowling trophy that he said was awarded almost every year, except for the years that people had it packed away and then couldn't find it until they cleaned out their garage.

"Now's our chance," I said.

Slowly and carefully, Bud and Skip and I backed

away from the crowd, so we could sneak into the bushes where we'd hid Mayor Swagg's red bowling ball.

"Ya sure we can do it, Trig?"

"I'm sort of sure."

"We'll get caught."

"No we won't. Every soul in town is gathered down at the other end of the park. So while they're all around the bandstand, us Junior G-men can slip this old ball into where it'll do the most good."

"Hurry," said Skip.

Grabbing the red bowling ball, we ran like a trio of jackrabbits, heading toward the big cannon that Marvin Fillput had loaded up with gunpowder.

"I hope it fits, Trig."

"Likewise," I said.

My hands were getting sweaty. While I lifted up the bowling ball to stuff into the barrel, Skip and Bud pushed and yanked, trying to aim the cannon in what we hoped would be the worst possible direction. I left the ball stuck in the barrel and went back to supervise the cannon's aim.

"Left," I ordered.

"Is that enough?" grunted Bud.

"Well, it could be sort of too much. Bring her around to the right a nudge or two. Stop. No, it was better the other way."

Squinting one eye, I sighted; Bud and Skip tugged, their faces getting redder than the old cannon. Finally it was just near perfect. Right on target.

"Hey," said Bud from around front.

"What's the matter?" I asked.

"Ya know, Trig, you didn't push the bowling ball in far enough."

"My arm's too short. It's in as far as I can push it."

"We need something to push it in farther. Somebody is bound to spot it."

"What's that long thing called?"

"A ramrod," I said.

"Yeah," said Skip, "we need a ramrod. And fast."

At the other end of the park, everyone suddenly clapped hands and shouted for the winner of the bowling trophy. Folks threw their hats into the air.

"We don't have time," said Skip.

Then I saw what might save the day. Or ruin it, depending on whose side you were on, Mayor Swagg's or Pop Copperskittle's.

"That's it," I said, pointing at Herb Lester's long ladder that still leaned up against Miss Ivy Ransom's Boarding House. The upper end of the ladder led to Miss Beekin's window.

Up the ladder I went, faster than I had ever climbed anything in my entire life. I found what I was looking for, borrowed it, and climbed down again, holding the handle in my teeth.

"A toilet plunger?" said Bud.

"Miss Beekin's red rubber toilet plunger," I said, "is just what we need to push a bowling ball into a cannon."

And it worked.

I returned the toilet plunger to Miss Beekin's room, and was climbing down the ladder, when Mr. Jenner spotted me. He pointed a lean finger up toward my general direction.

"Hey," he snorted, "come down from there. You stay away from that there ladder, hear? You'll fall and get hurt. And spoil our celebration."

"Sorry," I said. "I'll come right down, sir."

"Kids," said Mr. Jenner. "What this town needs is a stockade."

The big moment was coming; and so was the crowd, as all of Clodsburg trotted across the Town Square to witness the annual firing of our cannon.

"Swagg Day," said Mayor Swagg above the excited mumble of onlookers, "has its own historic meaning for each and every one of us. And so, without further ado, I shall now call upon former Private Marvin Fillput of the U.S. Field Artillery to step forward and discharge our big red cannon which he himself has primed and loaded." The mayor gestured with his bandaged thumb.

"Cover your ears, folks," said Marvin.

Obediently, the hands of Clodsburg covered the ears of Clodsburg as Mr. Fillput, sweaty shirt and all, lit a match to the small torch that he had prepared for this very function. Somebody with a camera took Marvin's picture.

All eyes were on Marvin Fillput in his World War uniform, all except the eyes of Doris Jessup who was once again looking into the front end, the dangerous end. The crowd screamed in horror as Marvin didn't seem to take notice that Doris was peeking into the cannon.

"There's something inside," said Doris.

"Get away from there," yelled Mayor Swagg.

"But," said Doris, "it's a ball. Made out of red marble with two little holes."

57

"Oh, NO!" cried Mayor Swagg.

"Everyone back," said Marvin Fillput, waving his torch dangerously close to the cannon's touchhole. Doris ran like a November turkey.

"Stop him," yelled the mayor.

"Now?" asked Marvin.

"Please," screamed our worried Mayor Swagg, "please . . . not . . . NOW."

"Okay," said Marvin, "I'll wait." The burning torch was suspended in his hand. "Now?"

That was the very moment I pulled back the lever to cock my genuine Melvin Purvis official Junior G-man machine gun. For some reason, my finger just sort of squeezed the trigger:

BRRAATT-TAT-TAT-TATTT.

Mayor Swagg fainted into the arms of Miss Beekin who spilled open her pocketbook. Pills, in a variety of colors, rolled and bounced happily into the crowd. She shrieked, causing Jason to bare his fangs and bite Marvin Fillput who dropped his torch. Onto the cannon.

KA-BOOOOMMM.

Because of the big cloud of yellow smoke, I never saw Mayor Swagg's red bowling ball hit the new traffic light, but several said that it did. And so that's how the first red light in Clodsburg blinked its last.

Pop got his job back, but Melvin Purvis never did answer my letter.